D1650695

For Amy and Joe

D. M.

To Scott and Joan for all their work

V. G.

All for Pie, Pie for All by David Martin, illustrated by Valerie Gorbachev. Text copyright © 2006 by David Martin. Illustrations copyright © 2006 by Valerie Gorbachev. Reproduced by permission of the publisher, Candlewick Press, Inc., Cambridge, MA.

Houghton Mifflin Edition

No part of this work may be reproduced or transmitted in any form or by any means, electronic or mechanical, including photocopying or recording, or by any information storage or retrieval system without the prior written permission of the copyright owner unless such copying is expressly permitted by federal copyright law. With the exception of nonprofit transcription into Braille, Houghton Mifflin is not authorized to grant permission for further uses of this work. Permission must be obtained from the individual copyright owner as identified herein.

Printed in China

ISBN 13: 978-0-618-96018-7
ISBN 10: 0-618-96018-X

2 3 4 5 6 7 8 9 SDP 16 15 14 13 12 11 10 09 08

All for Pie, Pie for All

David Martin

illustrated by Valeri Gorbachev

Grandma Cat made an apple pie.

Little Brother Cat ate a piece.
Big Sister Cat ate a piece.
Momma Cat ate a piece.
Poppa Cat ate a piece.
Grandma Cat ate a piece.

One piece of pie was left.

And then the cats took naps.

"I smell apple pie," said Grandma Mouse.

Little Brother Mouse ate a piece.
Big Sister Mouse ate a piece.
Momma Mouse ate a piece.
Poppa Mouse ate a piece.

Grandma Mouse ate a piece.
Six crumbs were left.

And then the mice took naps.

"I smell apple pie," said Grandma Ant.

Little Brother Ant walked away with a crumb.
Big Sister Ant walked away with a crumb.
Momma Ant walked away with a crumb.
Poppa Ant walked away with a crumb.
Grandma Ant walked away with a crumb.

One little crumb was left.

Then Baby Ant woke up from her nap.

"Pie!" said Baby Ant.

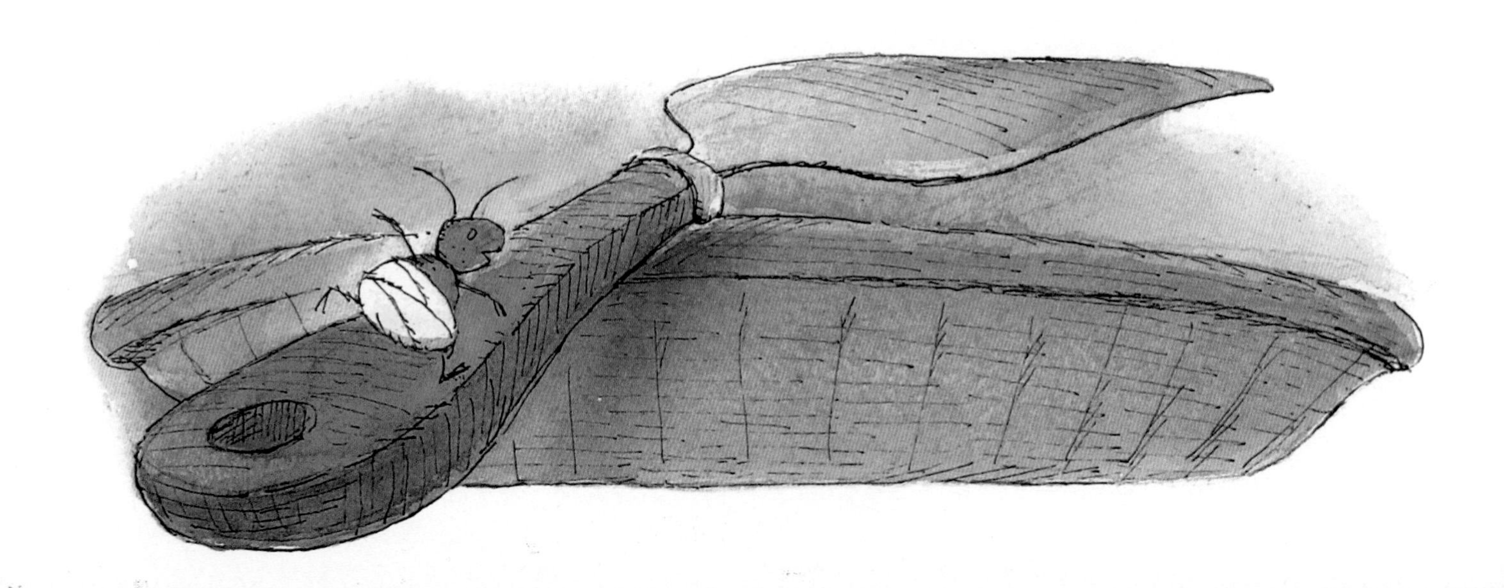

Baby Ant walked away with the last crumb.
Then the pie was all gone.

"I'm hungry. Should I bake another pie?" asked Grandma Cat.

"**Yes.**
Yes.
Yes.
Yes," meowed the cats.

"Yes. Yes. Yes. Yes. Yes," squeaked the mice.

"Yes. Yes. Yes. Yes. Yes. Yes,"

yelled the ants as loud as they could.

So Grandma Cat baked another pie.
This one was blueberry, and Brother Cat and Sister Cat and Brother Mouse and Sister Mouse and Brother Ant and Sister Ant and even little Baby Ant all helped make it.

SUGAR

And then everyone helped eat it,
until not even a crumb was left.